BEASTQUEST®

---> SPECIAL EDITION #2 <---

VEDRA AND KRIMON
THE TWIN DRAGONS

ADAM BLADE
ILLUSTRATED BY EZRA TUCKER

SCHOLASTIC INC.
New York Toronto London Auckland
Sydney Mexico City New Delhi Hong Kong

With special thanks to Allan Frewin

ISBN 978-0-545-39774-2

Beast Quest series created by Beast Quest Ltd., London.
BEAST QUEST is a trademark of Beast Quest Ltd.

Published by Scholastic Inc., 557 Broadway, New York, NY 10012, by arrangement with Working Partners Ltd.
SCHOLASTIC and associated logos are trademarks and/or registered trademarks of Scholastic Inc.

12 11 10 9 8 7 6 5 4 3 2 1   12 13 14 15 16 17/0

Designed by Tim Hall
Printed in the U.S.A.   40
First printing, July 2012

CHARACTER GUIDE

⊷ TOM ⊶

PREFERRED WEAPONS: Sword and magic shield

ALSO CARRIES: Destiny compass, jewel belt, and ghost map

SPECIAL SKILLS: Over the course of his Quest, Tom has gained many special items for his shield, giving him protection from fire, water, cold, and falling from heights, extra speed in battle, and magic healing ability. He also has the powers he gained from the golden armor, giving him incredible sight, courage, strength, endurance, sword skills, and energy.

⊷ Elenna ⊷

PREFERRED WEAPON: Bow & arrow

ALSO CARRIES: Nothing. Between her bow and her wolf, Silver, Elenna doesn't need anything else!

SPECIAL SKILLS: Not only is Elenna an expert hunter, she is also knowledgeable about boats and water. But most important, she can think quickly in tight spots, which has helped Tom more than once!

→ STORM ←

Tom's horse, a gift
from King Hugo.
Storm's good instincts
and speed have helped
Tom and Elenna from
the very beginning.

→ SILVER ←

Elenna's tame wolf and
constant companion. Not
only is Silver good to have
on their side in a fight,
but the wolf can also help
Tom and Elenna find
food when they're hungry.

⤙ ADURO ⤚

The good wizard of
Avantia and one of Tom's
closest allies. Aduro has
helped Tom many times,
but when Aduro was
captured by Malvel, Tom
was able to repay the
wizard by rescuing him.

⤙ MALVEL ⤚

Tom's enemy, determined
to enslave the Beasts of
Avantia and defeat Tom.
This evil wizard rules over
Gorgonia, the Dark
Realm. If he is near,
danger is sure to follow.

Welcome to Avantia. I am Aduro — a good wizard residing in the palace of King Hugo. I bring you a tale of a great Quest from Tom and Elenna's past — the birth of twin dragons, Vedra and Krimon.

The baby Beasts needed to make the journey to the neighboring kingdom of Rion where they could grow up in safety. But the evil wizard Malvel is never far away and the young Beasts needed protection, especially when a foe you may recognize showed up for the first time.

So how did Tom and Elenna protect Vedra and Krimon? You shall see. . . .

Yours,
Aduro

STORY ONE
⤙ TWIN BEASTS ⤚

⤚ CHAPTER ONE ⤛

A NEW PERIL

TOM STROKED HIS BRAVE STALLION'S NECK.

"Get well soon, Storm," he murmured. Tom's horse had been lamed on a rock, but was healing well in the palace stables. Tom's friend Elenna's pet wolf, Silver, lay in the straw at his side, refusing to leave Storm. "I have to go now," Tom told the animals. "But I'll come and see you again as soon as I can."

Tom left the stables, crunching through snow as he gazed up at the tall purple spires and the sea green domes of the Royal Palace. Frosty midwinter lay over the towns and villages, fields and forests of

Avantia. But in the Great Hall of the palace, a party was taking place to celebrate King Hugo's birthday.

Tom took a seat beside Elenna, her black hair a short-cropped tangle, her bow and quiver of arrows at her side on the bench. The hall was full of people eating and dancing to the music.

"A toast!" called one of the royal courtiers. "To King Hugo: Long may he reign!" There was a roar of approval and everyone raised their glasses.

Tom felt a rush of pride that he was a friend to the noble king. Elenna smiled and tapped her goblet against his. Then she leaned over and whispered into Tom's ear. "And to the Beasts of Avantia!"

"Shhh!" warned Tom. As far as most of the people of Avantia knew, the Beasts were just legend. It was the greatest secret in the realm that the old stories about the Beasts that protected the land were *true*! Tom and Elenna had seen the Beasts! And more than that — they had freed them from the evil power of the wizard Malvel.

But as Tom looked along the table, he thought it was strange that Aduro, the good wizard of Avantia, did not seem to be enjoying the party. The elderly man sat silently in his chair, wrapped in his faded red silk robes, his face solemn and his hand stroking his wispy gray beard.

The wizard turned and his gray eyes stared straight into Tom's.

"You are right," Aduro said with a grim smile. "I am troubled."

Tom had forgotten for a moment that the wizard had the power to read minds. Aduro pushed his chair back, rose, and came over to them. He rested his hands on Tom's and Elenna's shoulders.

"Come with me," he said quietly. "I have some news to tell you."

They got up from the table. Aduro parted a tapestry curtain and they slipped quietly out of the hall through a doorway. They found themselves in a little room with tall windows that looked out over the snow-covered town. Night had fallen and the town was bright with twinkling lights and the red glow of watch fires.

"Has something bad happened?" Elenna asked. "Are the Beasts in danger?"

Aduro gave her a mysterious look. "The Beasts you saved from Malvel's evil power are safe. But, elsewhere in our realm, something strange and wonderful has taken place. Something that happens only once in a thousand years." He leaned close, his eyes sparkling. "The forces that rule our world have created two new Beasts."

Tom gasped. "I didn't even know that was possible," he said. "What kind of Beasts are they?"

"Twin dragons, Vedra and Krimon," Aduro said. "Hatched from a single egg that lay hidden for centuries in the Caves of Nidrem."

"Baby dragons!" Elenna breathed. "Will we ever get to see them?"

The wizard's face was solemn. "That is why I brought you here." He drew himself up to his full height. "The birth of Vedra and Krimon could put the kingdom of Avantia in terrible danger once more."

He closed his hand around the jewel that hung from a thick chain around his neck. Tom saw a blue light shining out from between his fingers. The light hit the wall of the chamber. In the circle of light, Tom could see that the wizard had conjured a vision.

It showed a dark cave of sharp black rocks. At the back of the cave, Tom could see the broken shards of a thick white egg — an egg that must have been the size of a wagon when it had been whole.

Curious shapes lay curled on the floor of the cave.

"I can't make it out," Tom said, peering at the magical scene. "What are those green and red things?"

"Can't you guess?" Elenna said. "They're the dragons!"

"Oh! Yes!" Vedra and Krimon were curled up together, their wings and tails and long necks wrapped around one another. Their eyes were closed and thin streams of smoke drifted from their nostrils. Tom felt his heart lift at the sight of the newborn Beasts. They were magnificent and precious all at once.

"It is rare for two Beasts to be created at the same time," Aduro told them. He took his hand from the jewel and the vision faded away. "And, at this age, they are at their most vulnerable. If Malvel learns of their existence, he will do everything in his power to corrupt them."

"We'll protect the dragons," Tom vowed.

"We'll do whatever it takes!" Elenna added.

Aduro smiled. "I hoped you would say that," he continued. "But I must warn you, this will be a dangerous Quest, unlike any you have undertaken. You must be sure that you are up to the task."

Tom and Elenna looked at each other for a moment, then turned to the wizard.

"We are!" they said together.

CHAPTER TWO

THE DARK RIVER

THE WIZARD LED TOM AND ELENNA THROUGH a side door and down a long, winding stone stairway lit by flaming torches. Down and down the stairs went, and Tom realized with excitement that Aduro was leading them to the cellars that lay deep under the palace.

At last, the stairs ended and they followed the wizard through many dark cellar rooms while the sounds of the celebrations faded away far above them. Finally they came to a locked door. Aduro lifted his jewel pendant and touched it against the wood. The door sprang open.

He took a torch from the wall and led them into the room. It was small and round and quite bare except for a large wooden chest with metal straps that stood in the middle of the stone floor. A bundle of cloth lay beside the chest, and next to it were Tom's shield and sword, along with Elenna's bow and quiver of arrows. Aduro must have magically brought them here, so they'd be ready and waiting for them.

Tom looked around.

"Why have you taken us here?" he asked. "There's no way out."

Aduro looked at him. "Isn't there?" he said.

The wizard walked over to the chest and waved his hand over the curved lid. It flew open with a loud, startling clank.

Aduro picked up the bundle of cloth and then climbed into the chest. "Come, bring your things," he said.

Puzzled, Tom picked up his sword and the magic shield. It was decorated with powerful tokens from each of his previous Quests. It could save him from drowning and even protect him from fire. He climbed into the chest beside the wizard, leaving room for Elenna behind him with her bow and arrows.

Aduro stamped his foot twice and a panel in the bottom of the chest slid away to reveal a stone stairway that led down into utter darkness.

The wizard began to descend. Tom and Elenna exchanged a brief look and then followed.

The torchlight shone on the walls of the narrow stairway. Their footsteps echoed, but Tom could hear another sound. It was coming from below, an odd rushing sound that he almost recognized.

Dampness oozed from the walls, making the stones shine in the torchlight.

"I know that noise — it's running water!" Tom exclaimed.

"It is the hidden River Dour," announced Aduro as they came to the end of the steps. They found themselves by a wide, rushing underground river of black water. "This will take you to the very heart of the Caves of Nidrem, the sacred place where the Beasts gather and where none but the Master of the Beasts has ever set foot."

Tom had heard of the Caves of Nidrem, but they were the most sacred place in all of Avantia and he had never expected to go there. He frowned, realizing that they would have to go on this Quest without Storm and Silver. "Will you come with us?" he asked the wizard.

"This is your destiny, not mine," said Aduro. "Only you can enter the Caves of Nidrem."

Aduro led them along the rocky shore until they came to a place where a small rowboat was moored.

"The River Dour will lead you to the caves where the dragons hatched," the wizard told them. "Once there you must take Vedra and Krimon north, into the mountainous kingdom of Rion. There they will be safe from the evil reach of Malvel." His eyes glittered in the torchlight. "But beware — if the dragons are not taken to safety before the rise of the full moon, then Malvel will be able to cast his wicked spells over them."

"But what if Malvel gets to them first?" asked Tom. "Is there anything we can do to break the spells?"

"It would not be easy," Aduro said. "Let me see your sword."

Tom drew his sword from his belt and handed it to Aduro. This sword had helped him on so many adventures. It shone brightly in the torchlight. Aduro drew the blade up to his lips and whispered an enchantment. Tom's fingers tingled at the words.

"Your sword is now enchanted," Aduro said. "If Malvel has already put an evil spell on the Beasts, then the only way to set them free is for you to score upon their tender underbellies the symbol of Good." He looked at Tom. "It will take only a single touch, a light stroke from the tip of this blade," he said. "Enough to scar but not to wound. Only the steadiest of hands can make such a cut, and it must be done before the full moon has reached the very top of the sky . . . otherwise Malvel's spells will be unbreakable and Vedra and Krimon will be corrupted forever."

"I can do it," Tom said.

"Now, my friends," said Aduro. "It's time to go."

Tom and Elenna climbed down into the bobbing boat. The rush of running water was all around them.

"Take this," Aduro said, handing down the bundle. "It is food and drink for your long journey — and warm cloaks to keep out the cold. I know that your shield has Tartok's claw on it to protect you from cold, Tom, but the cloak will save you from getting soaked to the skin if it snows."

"Thank you, Aduro," Tom said, placing the bundle in the bottom of the boat.

"Farewell," said Aduro. "May your Quest be successful."

Tom looked up at the wizard from the prow of the boat. "While there is blood in my veins, I will do everything I can to keep Vedra and Krimon safe!" he said solemnly.

"And so shall I!" Elenna added, her eyes flashing.

"Then go, my brave friends," said the wizard, handing them the torch. He loosened the rope that held the boat to the shore. Elenna set the flickering torch in a holder in the prow and they sat side by side, each using an oar to bring the little craft out onto the belly of the dark river.

A sound came to their ears — a distant booming like sinister, mocking laughter.

"Malvel?" Elenna muttered.

"Yes, I think so," Tom said. He shivered. The River Dour was leading them into who-knew-what deadly dangers.

"Will we succeed again?" Elenna mused anxiously. "Can we defeat Malvel once more?"

Tom stared out over the prow of the boat.

"Don't worry," he said, trying to reassure her. "We've never failed before — and we're *not* going to fail now!"

⊷ CHAPTER THREE ⊶

THE TWIN DRAGONS

THE RIVER CHURNED ALL AROUND THEM. THEY
had been swept along on the dark water for hours.

"Oh no!" Elenna said, peering forward. Tom
looked. There was a thin line of whiteness in the
water ahead. The noise of the river had become
louder and more urgent.

"Rocks!" Tom gasped. "And the current is
pulling us toward them!"

The two friends dug their oars into the water,
fighting to turn the boat out of the path of the
rocks. Sweat ran down Tom's face, his muscles
aching as he thrust the oar into the water over and

over again. Tom knew that the splinter of Sepron's tooth that was fitted to his shield worked as a protection against fast-flowing water — but he wasn't so sure it would save them from these rocks! They were very close now. He could see them glistening in the torchlight.

"Come on!" Tom shouted. "We can do this!" He wasn't going to lose heart so early in the Quest. Gradually, the boat began to turn.

"We did it!" Elenna cheered as the first of the rocks slid by. But there were more sharp black rocks stabbing upward out of the swirling water. White foam broke against them as the river tried to dash their boat to pieces.

They rowed furiously, and at last they came through the rocks and were able to get their breath back.

"I hope this river doesn't have any more nasty surprises for us!" Tom gasped.

They became aware of a faint blue light far ahead — not daylight, but a soft blue glow that was like a steady flame.

As the light grew, they were able to make out the banks of the river and the ridged stone roof high above their heads. The blue light played on the water, getting brighter and brighter.

Their boat floated gently into a wide, calm lake under a high dome of rock.

"The light is coming from the rocks," Tom said. "And look! There's something in the water." He pointed.

A large shape was cutting through the water, sending up spouts of white foam. They recognized the Beast at once.

"It's Sepron!" Elenna shouted joyfully. The huge sea serpent was snaking through the water toward them, his scaly green body crested with a long fin and the seaweedlike mane streaming back from his head.

He opened his massive jaws and let out a deep, bellowing cry of welcome.

"Hello, Sepron!" Tom shouted. The Beast was huge — he swam around the boat, surrounding it with his long, shining coils. Then they saw the other Beasts gathered together on the shore.

Cypher the Mountain Giant came striding out into the water, his massive feet making loud rumbles with each step he took.

"Careful, Cypher!" Tom shouted up. "You'll swamp the boat."

None of the Beasts could speak, but Cypher gave a grunt as though he knew what Tom meant. He leaned down and gently picked up Tom and Elenna, then turned and waded back to shore.

The huge fire dragon Ferno lay under a cliff, his

black wings folded along his back, smoke drifting from his nostrils, his red eyes friendly. Tartok shambled forward, making welcoming snuffling sounds as she squatted down in front of the two friends. She reached out her two great hairy arms and pulled them into her fur. It felt to Tom as if he was being wrapped in a huge fleecy blanket until Tartok let them go again.

There was a loud croaking at their backs and they found themselves staring up into the fiery eyes of Epos the flame bird.

A mighty clopping of hooves announced the approach of Tagus the Night Horse. He reached down to Tom and Elenna, lifted them up with his human arms, and placed them onto his broad back.

He made a sound that was half speech and half neighing, and then he went cantering off along the glowing blue shore of the great underground lake with Tom and Elenna clinging to his back.

"Hang on tight!" Tom called to Elenna. He looked back and saw that the other Beasts were following. Tom felt good to be surrounded by all of his extraordinary and powerful friends.

They quickly came to a large cavern. A little way off, the stone floor sloped upward and they could see daylight — it was the way out of the Nidrem Caves! Tom and Elenna jumped down from Tagus's back.

The two newborn dragons lay together in a nest of golden straw. One was emerald green, the other red as a ruby. Their trusting eyes gazed at Tom and Elenna, white steam rising from their nostrils.

"That's why the Beasts are all here together," Tom said to Elenna. "They're protecting Vedra and Krimon."

Even newly hatched, the two Beasts were twice Tom's height.

"We're here to help you," he said soothingly as he approached them. He realized they didn't know what he was saying but the Beasts often seemed to understand the meaning behind his words.

Vedra, the green dragon, let out a nervous hiccup of excitement and a small spurt of red fire belched from between his jaws.

"Oh! They're wonderful!" Elenna said, reaching out her arms to the Beasts. The two dragons clambered out of the straw and moved forward unsteadily, their wings scraping the floor, their necks stretching out as they made little sounds in their throats.

Tom patted the hard, shining scales on Vedra's neck, allowing the Beast to cuddle up against him. He was aware of a faint burning smell, like the smoldering embers of a fire. He felt awed by the baby dragons, but also strangely protective of them. He knew he had a duty to keep them safe!

Krimon was standing in front of Elenna, gently nuzzling at her hair, a low rumbling sound coming from his belly, as if he was purring in contentment.

"They're so trusting," Elenna said, looking at Tom with concern. "Malvel mustn't be allowed anywhere near them!"

Tom looked at the other Beasts, gathered in the cave mouth.

He turned to Elenna. "Do you think they know what we have to do?" he said.

"Even if they do, how are we going to get the dragons to Rion?" Elenna asked. "How far is it — and how will we know when we're there?"

Before Tom could reply, he felt a tingling against his chest. Puzzled, he pulled out the magic map Aduro had given him when he had started his very first Quest. It was not flat like an ordinary map; it was alive! Snow-covered mountains rose up in sharp points from the parchment and Tom knew that if he touched the blue threads of the rivers, his fingers would be wet. The map had led the way to all his previous adventures, spinning out paths to guide him.

There was something new on the map! To the north of the palace, it glowed with a tiny point of golden light. He looked closer. The light was the cave mouth, and from it a slender golden path was spreading out, pointing the way north.

As he watched, the northern limits of the map began to expand beyond the boundaries of Avantia. New mountains rose up from the white parchment. There were new rivers and forests as well, and Tom realized that the map was changing to show him the snowy land of Rion.

He frowned. "It's a long way," he said.

"And Malvel could be following us," Elenna added.

Tom shivered. How could they possibly hope to get all the way to Rion without the evil wizard tracking them down and putting a spell on the young Beasts? And time was not on their side. The full moon was going to rise tonight — if Vedra and Krimon were not hidden in Rion by then, the Quest would fail!

Aduro had been right — this was going to be their greatest challenge yet!

CHAPTER FOUR

FLYING NORTH

Tom looked at Elenna. "We should go — as quickly as possible."

"I'll get the rest of the food and the cloaks Aduro gave us," Elenna called as she leaped onto Tagus's back and galloped over to the boat.

Tom looked at the baby dragons. They were sitting on their haunches, watching him with curious, innocent eyes.

"Please try to understand me," Tom told them. "You must come with us. You will be in terrible danger if you stay here." They blinked at him.

"There is an evil wizard who wishes to hurt you!" Tom said.

Vedra and Krimon shifted uneasily, as though they sensed the urgency in his voice.

Tom tapped his hand against his chest. "I am here to protect you."

"*We* are here to protect them, you mean," said Elenna, riding up behind him with the bundled cloaks in her arms. "Well, let's see if they understand," she added, hopping off the horseman. "Come on, little dragons — follow us!" She began walking toward the mouth of the cave.

To Tom's delight, the baby dragons got up and began to walk along behind them.

The other Beasts followed, too. They soon arrived at the wide cave mouth and found themselves staring out over a landscape of snow-covered hills and forests. This was a part of the kingdom Tom had never seen before.

The sky was clear and the dawning sun was low on the eastern horizon. Tom knew they must be a long way from the Royal Palace, but the map showed them that they still had a great distance to travel.

Tom and Elenna put their cloaks on. Sepron had stayed in the lake, but the other Beasts were congregated around them, as if to say farewell.

"We have to go now," Tom said to the Beasts.

Ferno and Epos stepped forward.

"What is it?" Elenna asked. Cypher picked her up, and Tartok picked Tom up. Tom's head spun as he was swung up onto Epos's feathery back. Elenna was placed astride Ferno's scaly neck.

"Of course!" Tom said. "They know we don't have much time to get to Rion. It would be impossible to fulfill the Quest without them!"

"But what about Vedra and Krimon?" Elenna said. "I know they've got wings, but we can't expect them to fly all the way; they're far too young."

Ferno turned his vast head to where Vedra and Krimon stood and made some deep rumbling sounds in his throat.

The baby dragons moved at once, Krimon clambering awkwardly up Ferno's wing onto the great dragon's back behind Elenna, and Vedra climbing onto Epos's back, cuddling up into the long, warm feathers just behind where Tom sat.

With a heavy flapping of wings, Ferno and Epos rose into the air. The snowy landscape fell away beneath them. Ferno and Epos circled the cave mouth once, where the other Beasts stood, proudly gazing up at them.

"Good-bye!" Tom called, reaching around to check that his shield was firmly in place on his back. The next moment, he needed both hands to cling to Epos's feathers as the great bird made a long curving swing upward and northward. Tom looked over his shoulder. Vedra was pressed tight onto Epos's back, his eyes wide with wonder as he stared down at the passing countryside.

"Malvel won't catch us now!" Elenna called.

"I hope not!" Tom called back.

They flew silently over the wintry landscape, the smooth blanket of snow shining like silver under the sun. It was early afternoon when Tom saw high mountains approaching under a sky thick with snow clouds.

Soon, they were beneath the clouds, flying through snow that filled all the sky. Their breath came out as mist, but Aduro's cloaks kept them snug and warm.

They flew over a jagged-toothed region of hills and crags. Tom pulled out the map and cleared the snowflakes out of his eyes. A golden glow showed their position. They were still in Avantia, but the border of Rion was fast approaching. It would not be long now!

Then Tom saw something odd on the map. He brought the parchment up closer to his face. One of the mountains on the map was different from all the others. It had a crater that was glowing with a fierce red fire.

"There's something strange ahead!" Elenna called.

Tom lifted his eyes. Right in front of them was the mountain that he had been looking at on the map.

"It's a volcano!" Tom shouted. "And it's erupting right in front of us!"

Epos let out a croak of alarm as a flood of molten rock and boiling smoke gushed up into the air. Tom saw that Elenna and Krimon were only just able to hold on to Ferno's back as he swerved away to the left to avoid the scalding fountain of fire.

A moment later Tom was almost wrenched from his place as Epos tried to avoid the huge flaming lumps of rock that were coming down in a deadly scorching rain. Vedra cried out behind him, clinging on fiercely to Epos's feathers.

Tom saw a fiery thunderbolt plunging toward them. He leaned back toward the baby dragon, throwing his shield up above his head in a desperate attempt to save them both.

Was the Quest going to end before it had begun?

CHAPTER FIVE

THE BOY ON THE MOUNTAIN

THE RED-HOT THUNDERBOLT BOUNCED OFF Tom's shield, hissing and spitting. The magical dragon scale in the shield had saved them! Tom's arm ached, but he kept the shield steady, while Vedra cowered behind him, shivering and whimpering in fright.

Tom saw Elenna clutching on to Ferno, the terrified Krimon squawking behind her as the huge Beast struggled to get clear of the volcano. But as Ferno turned, Tom saw Elenna's bow and quiver of arrows fall, spinning downward until they were lost in the flaming crater.

Epos gave a caw of alarm as she tried to pull away from the fiery mountain. The bird's body tilted as she swung left. Tom felt himself slipping. He had been so intent on keeping Vedra safe from the rain of fiery rock that he was not holding on tightly enough.

"No!" he cried as he slipped from Epos's back. The sky and the mountains wheeled around him. He saw the flame bird above him, her wings beating fiercely.

I've failed, Tom thought as he plunged helplessly downward through the icy air.

A wild rushing sound filled his ears, like a racing wind. A moment later, all the breath was jolted from his body. Epos had swooped under him, catching him with a triumphant caw.

Tom gasped, dizzy from his rescue. Dazed, he crawled up to sit between Epos's wings. "Thank you!" he shouted. He looked over his shoulder.

The green dragon was nodding his head and making chirping noises, glad that Tom had been rescued.

Ferno came swooping close.

"I lost my bow and arrows," Elenna called unhappily. "I can't believe they're gone!"

"Yes, I saw," Tom shouted. "It can't be helped. Let's get away from this volcano — then we can take a rest and figure out what we're going to do."

They flew on until the red glow of the volcano was far behind them. Tom peered down, scouring the rugged landscape for somewhere to land.

"Down there!" he called, pointing to a large flat slab of rock on a low ridge between the mountains.

Epos and Ferno circled down and landed. Tom spotted something at the far end of the slab of rock — something small and curled up. A sleeping animal, maybe.

He jumped down from Epos's back and went over to investigate. Elenna followed. "What is it?" she asked.

"It's a boy!" gasped Tom, stopping in surprise a few steps away from the curled-up shape. "What's he doing here all on his own?"

"Let's find out," Elenna said, running ahead of him.

"Be careful," Tom warned. He could hear an uneasy rumbling in Ferno's throat, and Epos was cawing nervously. Vedra and Krimon were staring at the boy and shivering. Something was wrong. The boy was wearing only light clothing, but the wind was raw and cut to the bone. How could he be sleeping in such a remote place as this? It didn't make sense.

"I don't think you should wake him," Tom said, coming up behind Elenna. "We have to get going."

But Elenna crouched at the boy's side and shook his shoulder.

"Hey! Are you all right?"

The boy's eyes snapped open and he jumped to his feet, his ice blue eyes strangely alert. Elenna stumbled back in surprise at the sudden movement. The boy stared at Tom, a thin smile spreading across his narrow pale face.

Tom looked at him. Those eyes were oddly familiar. As they stood staring at each other, cold threads of mist curled across the barren rock, making Tom shudder.

"My name is Seth," the boy said, his smile widening as he thrust out a hand toward Tom. "Who are you?"

Uncertainly, Tom reached out his own hand. "I'm Tom, and this is —"

He got no further. The boy's eyes flashed and

the smile turned to a grimace as he lunged forward, grabbing Tom's arm with both hands.

Tom let out a yell of shock as the boy half-turned, pulling Tom's arm so that he staggered off balance and was thrown headlong over the boy's shoulder.

He came crashing down on his back onto a rock with a cry of pain. He felt dizzy and disoriented and his eyes swam. He heard Elenna shout something.

He stared up at the white sky, gasping for breath. The boy loomed over him, and now Tom saw that he had a bronze sword in his hand, the point aiming for Tom's throat.

"And now that we have been introduced," the boy snarled, "I'm going to kill you!"

Tom stared up, helpless, as the blade rose and then plunged down toward him.

→ CHAPTER SIX ←

MAGIC DUST

TOM TWISTED TO ONE SIDE AS THE POINT OF the bronze sword struck the rock close to his head, filling his vision with sparks. Seth grunted with frustration as he stumbled forward. Tom sprang quickly to his feet, drawing his own sword and turning to face his foe, his shield up to defend himself.

"Why are you attacking us?" Tom asked, but Seth had spun on his heel. Bringing his blade up, he lunged forward with a snarl.

Tom used his sword to turn aside Seth's blade so that he could come in under the boy's arm and throw him off balance with a thrust from his shield. But Seth was too good a swordsman to be defeated by such a simple strategy. He bounded back, swinging his sword in a wide arc.

More sparks flew as their swords met with a clash, the noise echoing among the mountain peaks that surrounded them. Tom was aware of Ferno moving closer and of Epos watching with bright, angry eyes.

"Watch out!" Elenna shouted as the bronze sword came slicing through the air at neck height. Tom fended it off with his shield and thrust hard with his own blade. Seth leaped to one side, beating at Tom's weapon, almost smashing it from his grip.

Tom realized that Seth was his equal in strength, and also a very dangerous fighter. He would have to do something unexpected if he was going to win.

Tom risked everything in one big gamble. He let Seth beat him back step after step across the rock. He could hear Ferno rumbling in concern as he gave the impression that he was weakening. Epos cawed and Elenna let out a cry as Tom stumbled and fell onto his back.

Seth yelled in triumph and raised his sword high. But Tom had been faking his weakness. He twisted, scissoring his legs, slicing Seth's feet from under him. Seth fell with a howl and Tom was up and on him in a moment. He kicked the bronze blade out of Seth's grip and stood over him, panting as he pointed his sword at the boy's throat.

"Oh! Well done, Tom!" Elenna shouted, running up to them. She stared down at the grimacing boy angrily. "Why did you do that? We weren't going to hurt you!"

The cold fire faded from Seth's eyes and a look of bewilderment came over him. "I'm so sorry!" he

gasped, bringing his hands up over his face. "I didn't mean to hurt you. I didn't know what I was doing."

Tom glared down at him. "What are you talking about? You attacked me for no reason!"

"I was half-crazy with hunger and fear," said the boy. "I'm lost in this terrible place, and I haven't eaten for days. I thought you were a demon coming to murder me." He wiped his hand over his face. "I am truly sorry."

Tom frowned, confused by Seth's change of behavior. "You really expect us to believe that you didn't know what you were doing?" he asked.

"Please," begged Seth, "I've been hallucinating with hunger. I meant you no harm." He looked so pathetic and frail at that moment that Tom and Elenna exchanged a wary nod, deciding to give him another chance.

"You poor thing," Elenna said. "Wait there. We have food and water." She ran over to Epos and pulled down their bag of provisions. Tom, still not quite certain that Seth's story was the truth, picked up the bronze sword and slipped it into his belt before he allowed Seth to get to his feet.

"How did you get here?" Tom asked, eyeing the boy warily as he ravaged through the food that Elenna had brought.

Seth chewed hungrily, speaking with his mouth full. "I was with a hunting party — we were looking for the wild goats that live in these mountains. They make good eating. But a heavy fog came down and I got separated from the others. I've been surviving on rainwater and scraps of plants for days now." He looked gratefully at Elenna. "I thought I was going to die up here, all alone on this barren rock. You saved my life."

"You're welcome," Elenna said. She looked questioningly at Tom.

"I hope you find your way home safely," Tom said. "But we have to go now."

Seth gazed at the Beasts. "You fly on the most extraordinary . . . *birds* . . . I have ever seen," he said, his voice amazed. "At least, one of them is a bird, I think — huge though it is. But surely the other is a dragon?" A sudden light of understanding came into his eyes. "These must be two of the legendary Beasts of Avantia. They're *real*! Are you their Master?"

"No," Tom said, flattered that Seth might think that he could be the Master of the Beasts. "But I am their friend."

A smile spread across Seth's face. "I always thought in my heart that the legends were true," he said.

"No one is supposed to know," Elenna said. "The Beasts should never be seen."

Seth nodded. "Of course not," he said. He put his hand to his heart. "Don't worry," he said. "I promise that I will never tell anyone about what I have seen in this place. On my word of honor!" He looked from Tom to Elenna. "But . . . I don't know how to get down the mountains from here. If you leave me, I'll die."

"We can't take you with us," Tom said. "We're on an important Quest."

"We have to find the land of Rion," Elenna added.

"I live in Rion, in a small village beyond the mountains," Seth said. "Take me close to my home and I promise not to speak of these magnificent Beasts to a living soul!"

Tom and Elenna looked uneasily at each other. Could they trust him? On the other hand, Tom thought, could they be so cruel as to leave him all alone in the mountains?

"You may ride with us," Tom said, making sure to add: "But only as far as your home village."

Seth bowed his head as if Tom were King Hugo. "Thank you."

They went over to where the Beasts were waiting. Tom climbed up onto Epos's back and reached down to help Seth up in front of him. He wanted to keep an eye on the mysterious boy. Krimon looked at the newcomer with curiosity. Seth reached out his hand as if to touch the Beast, but the red dragon belched a little fire and Seth snatched his hand back.

Soon they were airborne again, flying high over the mountains with the cool wind in their hair. Tom saw the landscape begin to change beneath them. The mountains gave way to rugged hills cloaked in snow-laden pine forests. Blue lakes glowed in the valleys and gushing rivers leaped from rock to rock in white waterfalls.

He took out his map. They were beyond the northern borders of Avantia now. For the first time in his life, Tom was outside his kingdom.

Epos turned her head as she surveyed the unfamiliar landscape. Tom could sense that the Beast was as unsure of this place as he was. And looking to where Ferno was flying alongside, the anxious light in the dragon's eyes told a similar story.

"We're in Rion," Tom called to Elenna. "We must find somewhere safe to land!"

Beneath them stretched a great dense forest of pines. Tom searched for a clearing or open space where the Beasts could set down. Fierce snow-filled winds swept back and forth, making the tall pines bend and sway, and forcing Tom to cling tightly to Epos's back for fear of being blown off.

"There!" Elenna called, pointing down. "We can land there!"

Tom stared down. Yes! There was a clearing in the forest just ahead of them. Elenna and Ferno swooped down, and Epos prepared to follow.

Tom smiled. Aduro would be pleased with them — they had brought Vedra and Krimon to safety without any sign of Malvel.

But then Tom felt Seth shifting in front of him. He looked over Seth's shoulder and saw the boy take a small leather pouch out of his jacket.

"What is that?" Tom asked.

Seth opened the bag and dipped his hand into it. Golden powder trickled from between his fingers. "It's magic!" he said, that familiar cold light burning in his eyes again. "The dark and deadly magic of Malvel!"

"No!" Tom shouted. But he was too late. Seth leaned forward and hurled the fistful of gold dust into Epos's eyes. The flame bird let out a deafening croak of rage and alarm, twisting and spiraling in the air.

Seth laughed and turned, hurling a second handful of dust into Tom's face. Tom tightened his legs around Epos — he couldn't protect himself. The golden powder filled his eyes, stinging badly and blinding him. He clawed at his eyes, horribly aware of the air rushing wildly past him as Epos plummeted headlong toward the ground.

CHAPTER SEVEN

MALVEL'S LAUGHTER

Epos hit the ground with a crash that shook the forest. Tom plunged blindly from her back. As he fell, he could hear Vedra crying out and Epos croaking in pain and rage.

Tom rolled helplessly across the ground, losing his shield and sword as he tumbled over and over. At last, he came to a skidding halt in thick snow. He lay on his back, gasping and dizzy. A dancing golden light filled his stinging eyes, blotting everything else out.

"Elenna!" he called. *"Elenna!"*

He got to his feet, staggering about, his hands

hitting against the trunks of trees, his nostrils filled with the scent of pine.

"I'm here!" called a familiar voice. "What happened? Did something hurt Epos?"

Tom grabbed hold of Elenna's arm. "It was Seth. He threw some dust in our eyes. It blinded us." Tom turned his head. "Where is he?" His voice became grim. "And where's my sword?"

"You can't fight him if you can't see," Elenna said, catching hold of Tom as he lurched toward the sound of Epos's caws. "Wait!" she said. "I can hear running water." She pushed Tom and he felt his back hit a tree trunk. "Stay right there!" she ordered. "I'll get water to wash your eyes."

Tom stood listening to the sounds of the troubled Beasts — Epos's angry croaking and the anxious rumbling of Ferno. He could also hear the frightened cries of a baby dragon. How could he have been so stupid as to allow Seth to come along with them?

"I'm back." It was Elenna's voice, and a moment later, icy water splashed in Tom's face. "Keep still!" Elenna told him as he flinched away from the water. "There," she said. "How's that?"

Cautiously, Tom opened his eyes. There was still a golden glow on the edges of his vision, but the pain was gone and he could see again.

"Where is he?" Tom said angrily. He set off at a run back to the clearing where the Beasts waited. As he moved, he scooped up his sword and shield, readying himself for battle. He noticed that Seth's bronze sword was missing from his belt. That was bad. The boy was armed again; but this time, Tom would show him no mercy.

Epos was shaking her head from side to side, trying to get the golden dust out of her eyes. Ferno stood protectively close by, fire playing at his nostrils and his eyes glittering angrily.

There was no sign of Seth.

As Tom and Elenna raced into the clearing, Krimon came creeping out from beneath Ferno's wing, where he had been hiding. He ran forward, his wings flapping weakly.

Tom looked into the baby dragon's pleading eyes.

"Where's Vedra?" Elenna gasped, staring around the clearing.

"Seth must have taken him," Tom said. Filled with guilt and anger, he ran into the middle of the clearing, swinging his sword in his helpless rage. He shouted: "Seth! You dirty coward! Come back here and face me!"

A deep, hollow laugh echoed across the treetops. It was a horribly familiar sound that made Tom's flesh crawl. He came to a sudden stop, his anger freezing.

"Malvel!" he shouted into the air. "I swear — I'll get the Beast back from you!"

Another gust of laughter shivered through the trees.

Malvel had outwitted him, and now the green dragon was under the evil wizard's thrall.

Snow began to flurry across the clearing. Elenna came up behind Tom.

"We've failed," she murmured. "Malvel has beaten us."

"No!" Tom said firmly, gripping his sword. "We'll get Vedra back." He looked at her. "We *will*!"

But as the blizzard grew worse, his heart was filled with doubt. They were in an unknown land, he had no idea how to start searching for Vedra, and there was still Krimon to protect.

He had brought the baby Beasts to Rion — at least he had fulfilled *that* part of the Quest. But he wondered what new challenges awaited him.

To be continued . . .

STORY TWO
⊷ DANGER IN RION ⊶

CHAPTER ONE

BLIZZARD

TOM STARED GRIMLY INTO THE HOWLING blizzard. How were they going to be able to track Seth and the lost Beast in such terrible weather?

Elenna stood at his side. "The full moon will rise tonight," she said thoughtfully. "We only have till then to rescue Vedra from Malvel."

Tom turned to look at Krimon, shivering at Ferno's side. Close by, Epos was huddled on the ground.

"Will Epos be all right?" Elenna asked.

Tom ran over to the injured flame bird. "I hope

so." He could see pain in the Beast's golden eyes. "But I don't think she'll be able to fly for a while."

Ferno crawled closer to Epos, lifting one black wing to shield the hurt flame bird from the blizzard. As the snow touched the great dragon's scaly hide, it turned to steam, so that the Beasts were shrouded in a cloud of fine mist. Krimon was huddled up against Ferno's side, mewling and staring around as though hoping that his brother would come trotting out of the snow at any moment.

Suddenly, the baby red dragon let out a sharp cry and stood up. He scuttled forward into the snow, making little calling sounds in his throat.

"Where's he going?" Elenna asked.

"I think he can sense his brother," Tom said.

Krimon headed toward the forest. He turned and looked back at them. Then he lifted his head and let out a small spurt of flame from his mouth. A wing lifted, beckoning to them.

He turned to the forest again, tilting his head as though listening. He let out a high-pitched growl and darted forward.

"We must follow him," Tom said.

"What about Epos and Ferno?" asked Elenna.

Tom turned and saw Ferno lift his black wing and curl it over Epos. Suddenly, all that could be seen was a huge black rock in the middle of the clearing.

"Just like when we first met him!" Tom said to Elenna. "Remember? He looked exactly like a part of the mountain. He's done the same thing again to keep them both safe." He turned to the forest. "I can't see Krimon anymore. We mustn't lose him!"

Tom and Elenna plunged into the dark and forbidding forest.

"Where has he gone?" Elenna asked, peering into the gloom.

Tom stared through the trees, but he could only see clearly for a little way and after that, all was black and grim. There was no sign of the baby Beast.

"We were too slow," Tom said in despair. "Krimon's gone!"

CHAPTER TWO

DRAGON FIRE

TOM RAN BETWEEN THE SNOW-LADEN TREES, calling out to the baby dragon.

"Hey! Come back!"

Elenna ran up to him and caught his sleeve. "Shhh!" she hissed. "Listen!"

There was a rustling sound in the trees.

"There!" Elenna yelled, pointing. A moment later, Tom saw Krimon trot into view.

The Beast stopped in front of them, eyes shining brightly, his head bobbing on his long neck.

"Do you know which way they went?" Tom asked.

The Beast's head tilted, as if he was trying hard to understand what Tom had said. He snorted and a flicker of flame came from his nostrils.

Elenna pointed into the trees. "Show us the way if you can," she said.

Krimon snorted again and turned back. He moved off through the trees, trotting along confidently, a low purring growl vibrating in his throat.

The dark trees towered threateningly overhead and shadows crowded around them. Tom gripped his sword — this was no ordinary forest!

Krimon paused on a snow-covered track and lowered his snout, sniffing the ground. Then he closed his eyes and lifted his head. A moment later, long bright flames streamed upward from his nostrils.

Tom watched in amazement as the tongues of flame hung in the air above the dragon's head, bathing the trees in ruby light, changing shape and weaving together until they became a bright red fireball that turned slowly in the air, hovering between the trees.

"What's he doing?" Elenna asked, backing away from Krimon.

"I don't know," Tom replied. "But look at his chest!" A gentle orange glow was growing on the red leathery skin just over where the Beast's heart must have been. As Tom and Elenna watched, the glow deepened and began to pulse — and in the center of the orange light, there was a small heart of emerald green light. A similar green light shone in the middle of the hovering fireball.

"It's beautiful," said Elenna. "But what does it mean?"

"I think it means that there's a bond between the two Beasts," Tom said. "They're linked in some way." He called to the dragon. "Go on and we'll follow." There was no time to waste — the moon would be rising soon.

With a snort, Krimon plunged into the trees. Tom and Elenna quickly caught up with him. All three of them pushed their way through the undergrowth, snow falling from the branches all around them, the fireball gliding along in front, and the orange and green light throbbing at the Beast's heart. Every now and then they heard the sinister sound of Malvel's mocking laughter, and the deeper they headed into the forest, the darker and more menacing it became.

As Krimon darted this way and that through the trees, Tom saw that sometimes the orange fireball would become dim and the green light would almost disappear. At other times the fireball would glow as brightly as a furnace, and Tom knew that they were heading in the right direction. But time was against them as the winter daylight faded.

"It will be dark soon," Elenna said, her breath white in the chill air. "We have to find Vedra before nightfall."

"Aduro said the Beasts would be safe until the full moon reached the top of the sky," Tom said urgently. "We're running out of time."

Krimon came to a sudden halt. Ahead of them, a great hedge of holly blocked the way, its branches as thick as Tom's arms, its spiky, leathery leaves shining eerily in the red light of the hovering fireball.

Tom looked at the prickly, snowcapped hedge. He was sure that it had been deliberately put across their path.

The baby dragon ran distractedly back and forth along the line of the hedge. As far as Tom and Elenna could see, the dense wall of holly stretched on forever in both directions. Mocking laughter echoed through the shadowy trees.

Krimon stood in front of the hedge. He lifted his head and let out a long, keening cry. Tom looked at his face and saw that great, shining, diamond-bright tears were running from his eyes.

His brother was on the other side of that massive hedge, but there was no way through.

CHAPTER THREE

THE LABYRINTH

TOM DREW HIS SWORD AND STEPPED UP TO the towering holly hedge, a grim determination building inside him. He was not going to be stopped from fulfilling his Quest. "Not while there is blood in my veins!" he muttered as he gripped his sword in both hands.

He swung with all the strength he had. The sword sliced through leaves and branches, sending them flying.

"Good work, Tom!" Elenna shouted. She dragged the twigs and branches away as he stepped forward

into the hedge, hacking at it while splinters of wood and spiky leaves flew about.

His muscles ached and he was soon breathing rapidly with the effort of battling the ancient holly — but he could see no end to the tangle of branches. Behind him he could hear Krimon snorting encouragement.

At last, he had to pause as exhaustion overcame him. His sword felt unusually heavy, and the muscles in his arms and shoulders were full of pain. He lowered his weapon, gasping for breath. A feeling of defeat overwhelmed him. "I don't know what's wrong with me," he said. "I've never felt like this before."

"We'll get through. It'll just take time, that's all."

Tom looked at Elenna. "We don't *have* time. It's already getting dark," he said. "You know what Aduro said — if Malvel puts his spells on the dragons when the full moon is at its height, they will be corrupted forever. They will be evil — and we won't be able to save them."

A snort made them both turn. Krimon was peering at them with sad, lonely eyes. The orange light at his chest was dim and the green heart of fire had almost vanished.

The dragon extended his long neck and gently took the collar of Elenna's tunic in his mouth.

"What's he doing?" she gasped as the dragon drew back, tugging her along with him and making urgent growling noises in his throat. "Hey! Careful!" she called as she was lifted off her feet and put to one side. "You want us out of the way? Is that it?"

Krimon released her and made a sharp, high-pitched croaking noise.

"Tom!" Elenna called. "Come out of there. I think Krimon has a plan."

Tom stepped out of the hole he had cut in the hedge. The dragon pushed his head into it. Tom saw his sides expand, as though he was taking a deep breath.

A moment later there was a roaring of fire, and a burst of red flame came pouring from the Beast's mouth and nose. Smoke billowed out of the hole and there was a sharp smell of burning. As Krimon moved forward into the hedge, clumps of snow fell from the upper branches, turning to thick white steam as they hit the flames.

The dragon pushed farther into the hole.

"He's burning his way right through!" exclaimed Elenna. "Good work, Krimon!"

Tom and Elenna followed the dragon into the scorched and smoldering hedge. The smoke made them cough, and they could hardly see a thing as they stumbled along behind the Beast, but it was not long before they were through the hedge and breathing fresher air.

Tom wiped his watering eyes with his sleeve. Beyond the barrier of holly, the forest looked quite different. There were no pine trees here, just endless parades of snow-laden holly bushes, tall as trees and as dense as the bush they had just fought their way through. Paths led through the ranks of trees, thick with untrodden snow.

"There are so many different pathways," Elenna said. She looked at Krimon, who was staring this way and that as though he was trying to find an elusive scent on the air. The glow on his chest was pale and the ball of fire that floated above his head had gone dim.

Elenna patted the dragon's neck. "Find him!" she said encouragingly. "I know you can do it!"

The Beast ran forward along one of the many paths. The fireball grew even fainter. He turned and ran back, following another path. This time the fireball began to glow more brightly.

"That's the way!" Tom said.

Paths led off to the left and right, and sometimes the main path forked and Krimon had to pause for a moment to decide which route to follow. But Tom could see the orange patch glowing bright on his chest, and the heart of green light shining out strongly. The fireball was throwing out sparks of red and green, bright and fierce.

Tom stared up into the sky. The snow clouds were gone and the sky was clear — pitch-black and sparkling with the cold glitter of winter stars. A deadly chill came creeping through the holly, and Tom was glad of the protective power of his shield as his breath clouded. Krimon did not seem to feel the cold, but he saw that Elenna was shivering despite her cloak.

"It can't be long now before the moon rises," he said to her.

"But look how bright the dragon fire is," she said. "We must be *very* close."

They came to another fork in the path. Krimon hesitated. A sudden burst of flame ignited close to Tom's head. He jumped back, his shield up and his sword ready in his hand.

Elenna gave a yelp of alarm as another flash of fire appeared on the other side of the pathway. Then more and more fires appeared, igniting one by one all along the path.

"They're torches!" Tom said in amazement, gazing at the long lines of bright lights that hung from the holly branches. "Look — they're everywhere."

"I don't like it," Elenna said. "It's as if the forest has come alive." She frowned. "This is dark magic.

These lights aren't here to help *us*." She turned. "Oh!" She backed away from the hedge.

Tom saw a large dark shape among the branches. Red eyes glinted. The torchlight gleamed off of raised claws and bared fangs.

"Get back!" Tom shouted, leaping in front of Elenna. A monstrous creature reared above him.

CHAPTER FOUR

THE EVIL CHARM

TOM RAISED HIS SWORD DEFIANTLY AS THE creature loomed over him in the torchlight. It was human-shaped and dark green. Its thick, shiny hide was covered in spikes, its claws as long as swords and its eyes like boiling blood. But then Tom realized the creature was not moving. Puzzled, he stepped forward.

"Be careful!" Elenna called.

Tom swung his sword so that the flat of the blade struck the creature's leg. There was a resounding clang. Tom turned, grinning. "It's just a statue!"

Elenna came to stand next to him. "It looks nasty," she remarked.

They saw that the hedges were filled with many hideous statues, grown over by the holly so that they were half-hidden.

Krimon was still at the fork in the maze, growling and whimpering to himself, his head turning to and fro.

"He doesn't know which way to go," Elenna said, walking over to the Beast.

Tom stared along the two pathways. They were exactly alike. He walked a little way along the left-hand path. A thick green mist swirled around his ankles, rising from the ground beneath his feet. Sudden, darting pains behind his eyes brought him to a halt.

"What's wrong?" asked Elenna.

"My head feels like it's in a vise!" Tom stumbled back. The moment he reached the fork, the green mist seeped back into the ground and the throbbing in his head faded away.

"I don't think it can be that way," Tom said, staring uneasily along the left-hand path. "At least, I *hope* it isn't."

Suddenly, Krimon seemed to make up his mind — and to Tom's relief, he went lumbering down the right-hand path. Tom was sure now that Vedra must be at the heart of this labyrinth.

He stared up at the inky sky. Stars twinkled frostily. The moon had not yet risen — but he dreaded at any moment to see it lifting above the snowy tops of the hedges.

They came to another fork. The left-hand path was narrow and heavily overgrown, but the red dragon pushed his way through, the prickly leaves scratching along his scales, the dislodged snow trickling down with a soft hiss.

Elenna followed, Tom close behind. But the moment Tom set foot on the path, a green mist filtered up out of the ground and swirled around his feet — and the headache returned.

"This can't be the way," he called. But above the Beast's head the fireball was pulsing strongly. Elenna paused, a worried look coming into her eyes as she saw the mist that drifted around Tom's feet.

"Krimon thinks it is," she said. "Is the pain very bad? Don't inhale any of that mist!"

Tom winced and tried to hold his breath as the throbbing got worse. If this was the way, then he would have to put up with the pain. "Don't worry about me," he said, hoping he sounded more confident than he felt. "Keep close to Krimon. I'll be right behind you."

Elenna turned and ran after the fast-moving Beast. Tom screwed up his eyes against the pain, covering his mouth with his hand, determined not to give up. A soft, low laugh sounded behind him. He turned. A hooded figure stood at the end of the pathway.

It was Malvel. The evil wizard's laughter rang in Tom's ears. An uncontrollable surge of anger burst through Tom at the sound of that hated voice. With a shout of rage, he ran back along the path, his shield up, his sword at the ready.

"Tom! No!" He ignored Elenna's warning. Malvel was within his reach. He had the chance to defeat the evil wizard once and for all.

Malvel stood at the fork in the paths, his head thrown back as his laughter rang up into the night sky. He pointed and laughed again. Tom followed the line of the pointing finger. The upper arc of the moon had just cleared the tops of the hedges, the moonlight reflecting eerily on the snow. Time was running out!

Elenna caught hold of Tom and forced him to stop.

"What are you doing, Tom? You're going the wrong way."

Tom thrust his sword in Malvel's direction. "I have to fight him!" he shouted angrily, trying to tear himself away from her.

"Fight who?" Elenna gasped. "Tom? There's no one there."

Tom stared at her. "Are you blind?" he shouted. "Malvel is standing right in front of us!"

"No, he isn't," Elenna insisted. "There's nothing there. It must be the headache and the mist — it's making you see things."

Tom dragged his arm free of her grip, overcome with an intense anger.

"You need to calm down," Elenna said gently.

Tom realized that he was almost panting with fury. What was wrong with him? Had Malvel made himself invisible to Elenna — or was she right, and it was just an illusion?

He slowed his breathing and the anger started to disappear — and the shape of Malvel faded away to nothing.

Tom looked at Elenna. "Thank you," he said quietly. "Malvel must be using that green mist to try and control me. But what do I do if I can't trust my own eyes?"

Elenna took his shoulder. "Trust mine," she said. "Come on — we mustn't let the dragon get away from us."

They ran side by side along the path. The green mist was gone and now Tom's head felt much better.

Krimon was standing still, facing a great dark door that blocked off the path. The young Beast was keening and wailing softly. The door showed scorch marks where the dragon had tried to burn it, but the glossy wood was unharmed by his fire.

The orange glow was still bright on his chest, and the fireball flared above his head.

"This has to be the way," Elenna said. "We should look for a key, or some other way to get the door open."

"But there's no handle," Tom said, his anger flaring up again. He lifted his sword in both hands, smashing again and again at the dark wood. Splinters flew, but the door didn't move.

He hammered his shield into the wood, pounding with the hilt of his sword.

"Tom, stop!" Elenna called. "That can't be the way!"

Tom ignored her, letting out a howl of rage as he made one last effort, kicking at the door with all his strength. It swung open on creaking hinges. Tom glared at Elenna. "See!" he shouted. "I did it!

I knew I could get it open!" Wild elation filled him as he shoved his way through the door. But all that met him was another snow-covered path.

"No!" Tom cried. He ran from side to side, beating at the hedges with his sword. "I hate this place!" he screamed.

Krimon backed away from him as though Tom had become something to fear.

Elenna darted forward and caught Tom's sword arm. "Get off me!" he snarled, wrenching his hand free. He lifted the sword and was about to bring the blade down on her head when he looked into her eyes and realized what he was doing.

With a cry of alarm and horror, he staggered back a few steps. Then he threw his sword down, and fell to his knees.

"I'm sorry!" he gasped. "I'm so sorry!"

Elenna knelt in front of him, her hands on his shoulders.

"Look at me, Tom," she said firmly.

He gazed into her eyes, his chest heaving and his limbs shaking.

"This isn't your fault," she said. "Something has been done to you. It's making you behave in this way." Tom heard fear in her voice. "Tom — I think that the dust that Seth threw in your eyes has put you under an evil spell. You have to fight it, Tom. You have to fight it really hard — if you don't, then Malvel will win."

Tom could barely speak. He didn't know what to do. This Quest was too hard. Everything felt hopeless.

CHAPTER FIVE

THE CHASM

"I CAN'T CONTROL MYSELF," HE SAID. "MALVEL'S magic is too strong! I can't beat him, Elenna. I can't!"

"You have to try," Elenna said. "I'll help you."

"But you don't understand — What if I attack *you*?"

"You think you can take *me*?" Elenna said, arching an eyebrow. "Don't be so sure!"

Krimon was still eyeing Tom nervously, as though he could sense the evil charm. "Don't be scared, I'm better now," Tom said, hoping that he would be able to control his rage.

"Come along," Elenna called to the Beast. "Let's go and find your brother!"

With a snort, Krimon pushed through the open doorway and went trotting along the pathway.

Following, Tom glanced up at the sky. Half of the full moon was visible now over the holly hedges. They had so little time.

They had not been going for long before they came to a wide chasm that stretched across their path. Krimon stood at the edge, peering over to the far side.

Tom stared down into the chasm. It was very deep, and far, far below them he could see flames flickering. He knew the tokens in his shield would protect him from the fall, but that would be no help to Elenna.

"We have to get across," he said.

"I know. But how?"

While they were still wondering what to do, the dragon took a few steps backward and then leaped across the chasm. His wings spread as he landed safely on the far side. He turned, looking back at them.

"Come back!" Tom called. "You can carry us over."

Krimon snorted and let out a belch of flame. He clawed at the ground and turned his head, indicating that he wanted them to go with him.

"It's too far!" Elenna called. "You have to jump back and help us."

But Krimon did not understand; he just stood there watching them with a confused expression. Tom felt tears sting his eyes. He wished that they had not left Epos and Ferno behind; the two grown Beasts could easily have carried them over the chasm on their backs.

Tom fought hard to keep down his anger. It wasn't the baby dragon's fault. But they had to get across.

A thought struck Tom. "If we had a pole, we could vault over," he said.

"A branch from the hedge might work," Elenna agreed eagerly.

Tom ran to the holly hedge and hacked at it with his sword. He sliced off the smaller twigs and branches from one long limb, cutting it free and dragging it onto the path. He trimmed the long branch so that it became a smooth pole twice his own height.

He tested it. It seemed flexible enough not to break. "I'll go first," he said. "Then I'll throw it back for you."

He lifted the pole and rested it on his shoulder, taking several steps backward, his eyes fixed firmly on the far side of the chasm. He ran forward. The pole hit the ground. It slipped a little on the snow, then held firm. He sprang into the air, twisting in midair, propelling himself forward. He hung in the air over the chasm, glancing fearfully down to see the deep gulf gaping to swallow him. He gave a final jerk of his hips, the balance shifted, and he was safe on the other side.

He threw the pole back to Elenna and she caught it easily. A few moments later she was at his side.

"Let's hope that was the last obstacle," she said.

They walked on, but Tom quickly noticed that something was wrong with Krimon.

The Beast would falter every now and then, lifting a foreleg and rubbing at his neck with his claw, whining as if in pain. As they went on, Krimon got more and more distressed until finally, at a place where seven paths led off, he fell to the ground, tearing and scratching frantically at his neck.

"What's wrong with him?" Elenna asked.

Tom ran forward and fell to his knees beside the writhing dragon. "It must be the link to his brother," Tom said, panic rising in him. "Something bad must be happening to Vedra." He looked at Elenna. "Krimon is suffering the same pain!"

The dragon thrashed about on the ground, crying out in agony. Above the maze of hedges, the moon was rising in the sky, its cold light giving the snow a ghostly sheen.

Suddenly, the fireball over Krimon's head sputtered and went out, and at the same moment the orange glow on his chest disappeared. The Beast stopped writhing. He lay panting for a few moments, then got to his feet. Tom saw the look of loneliness in his eyes. Krimon began to whimper, thrusting his huge head into Elenna's shoulder, fat tears running from his eyes as she wrapped her arms around him.

"The link between Vedra and Krimon has been broken," Tom said. "Something very bad must have happened to his brother." He felt desperate. He had failed. This really was the end — without the red dragon to guide them, how would they ever get into the heart of the maze?

THE HEART OF THE MAZE

"**W**HAT ARE WE GOING TO DO?" ELENNA ASKED. Tom could see tears shining in her eyes as she cradled the Beast.

"Why ask me?" he snapped. "I'm not a wizard who knows everything!"

Elenna bit her lip.

"I'm sorry," he said, breathing deeply. He knew he had to fight against the anger. It would only cloud his mind and make things more difficult. But the whimpering of Krimon was making his head ache.

The dragon cried out again. Tom turned to the Beast, shaking, his hand on his sword hilt as he snarled, "Be quiet!"

"Tom, he isn't making a sound," Elenna said.

Tom stared at her. "I can hear him," he said. "He's howling and moaning."

"No, he isn't."

Tom looked at Krimon. The red dragon was perfectly still and calm. Then where was the whimpering and crying out coming from?

A sudden understanding dawned. "It's Vedra!" he gasped.

"I can't hear anything," Elenna said.

"I can — listen closely. There!" Tom said. He stared around the junction of the seven paths. Facing one of them, he heard Vedra's cries grow louder.

"He's this way!" he said. "Come on — try to get Krimon to follow."

Tom ran down the path, filled with new faith in himself. Seth had put an evil charm on him to try and make him fail — and now that same charm was leading him to the Quest's end.

Elenna and Krimon followed as Tom ran through the maze, kicking up clumps of snow as he went. His breath was white smoke in the freezing night air. Krimon's voice was loud now — the lost Beast was very close.

The full moon had risen above the hedges and was shining down into the labyrinth of snow-laden holly trees. But they still had a little while before it reached the top of the sky. Time to succeed . . . or time to fail.

Tom came to a fork in the maze.

"I can hear him now," Elenna cried, coming up behind him as he hesitated at the junction.

With Tom in the lead, they turned a final bend and came stumbling into a wide circular clearing.

Vedra was there in the center — pinned to the ground by thick spiked chains of gold. As the Beast struggled, the spikes tore his flesh, and Tom saw that the injuries were worst around Vedra's neck, where threads of blood ran down his shining scales. Tom realized that these must be the injuries Krimon was feeling.

Standing just out of reach of the dragon was Seth. The boy smiled as Tom and Elenna and Krimon came into the clearing.

"I see you have come to watch the full moon with us," Seth said with a mocking bow. "My master hoped you would be here in time to see the Beasts corrupted."

Tom was about to launch himself at the smirking boy, when Krimon ran past him toward his captive twin.

To Tom's surprise, Seth took a sudden sidestep toward Vedra and jerked at the end of his chains.

The golden links fell away from the Beast and he rose from the ground.

But Tom could see that something had happened to the green dragon. As his twin ran forward, Vedra reared up, his eyes gleaming with wicked magic. His jaws opened and a burst of fierce red fire spurted toward Krimon. A moment later, Vedra leaped at his brother, roaring with anger, his jaws wide, his claws raised.

Malvel's dark magic was in Vedra's blood — he had already been turned to evil. Tom was too late.

CHAPTER SEVEN

THE FULL MOON

WITH A CRY OF RAGE, TOM RUSHED TOWARD Vedra to stop him from attacking his twin. But Seth sprang forward, his bronze sword whirling in the moonlight. "You can't do anything now. Vedra is ours!"

"Try fighting me one-on-one," Tom challenged his opponent. "No magic tricks."

Seth grinned, his face pure evil. "I don't need magic to defeat you." Quick as a snake, Seth struck out with his bronze sword and sent Tom's blade leaping from his hand.

Tom fell back as blow after savage blow rained

down on his shield. He stumbled down onto his side in the snow, just managing to keep his shield up. Over to one side, he could see Vedra and Krimon engaged in their own ferocious fight.

Seth straddled Tom, his sword rising and falling. Tom felt his arm muscles weakening under the relentless assault. He could not think properly and despair and defeat were filling his mind.

Then he heard a high-pitched yell and above the rim of his shield he saw Elenna attacking Seth from the side, wielding Tom's own sword, beating Seth back, trading attacks as she forced him away from Tom.

But even as Tom tried to get to his feet, he saw that Elenna's attack was failing. Seth was too strong for her. He fought back with hard and fast strikes. Using all his strength, Tom hurled the shield, skimming it just above the ground. It caught Seth below the knees, sending him crashing.

Elenna was quick to take advantage of their enemy's fall. She brought her foot down on his wrist, stooping to snatch the bronze sword from his fingers.

"Well done, Elenna!" Tom shouted, scrambling to his feet.

"I've got him," Elenna called. "Take this — help Krimon!" She threw Tom his sword, transferring Seth's weapon to her right hand and aiming the point squarely at the sprawling boy's throat. Seth glared up at her but didn't try to move.

The noise of the fighting twin dragons was terrifying. Their roars filled the clearing as tails lashed and flame spurted and claws lunged. Vedra was winning the fight, the evil inside him making him fight more fiercely. As Tom ran forward, he saw Krimon tumble onto his back with a howl.

Vedra pounced on his twin with a blast of fire. The snow turned to spurting steam all around them. If it weren't for Krimon's scales, he would have been scorched to death by the blast of flame.

The fact that Vedra's attention was focused on his brother was Tom's only advantage. He knew what he had to do and with the moon high in the sky he had only a few seconds left to do it. He remembered Aduro's words. He had to score Vedra's underbelly with the tip of his sword, marking him with the sign of Good. And he had to do it before the possessed Beast noticed him.

He ran in close, looking for a way to get in under the green dragon's scaly sides. It was impossible! The soft underparts were too well protected.

The moon was a handbreadth from the top of the sky. Tom stared up at the silver disc for a moment, a plan forming in his mind. He hadn't come so far to give up now.

"Hey!" he shouted above the roaring of the dragons. He struck Vedra's foreleg with his sword.

The metal rang uselessly on the emerald scales, but the green dragon's fiery eyes turned toward him.

He leaped aside as a blast of flame burned the ground where he had been standing. He had to act quickly. He angled his shield, tilting it just so — holding its burnished face up to the sky so that the reflection of the full moon was caught on its shining surface.

He tilted it just a little more, seeing a flash of brilliant silver light strike Vedra in the eyes. Dazzled and blinded, the Beast reared up, his wings stretching wide. His jaws opened to spew a fountain of flame into the night sky.

Tom did not hesitate. He sprang forward, seeing the soft belly of the dragon revealed. He used the very tip of his sword, carefully scoring the sign of Good into the yielding flesh.

"No!" He heard Seth howling, but in an instant his voice was swallowed by a whirling sound like a thousand hurricanes. Tom stood firm, his eyes blinded by the racing winds that blasted across the clearing, his ears filled with the noise.

And then there was a long, deep silence. Tom opened his eyes. The maze of towering holly bushes was gone. He was standing on a plateau of deep, smooth snow. Vedra and Krimon were beside him, blinking and shaking their heads in confusion. Elenna was nearby, but Seth and the bronze sword were gone.

"You did it!" Elenna shouted.

"*We* did it!" Tom said with a grin.

The twin Beasts were recovering now, rubbing fondly up against each other and crooning. Vedra was cured of the evil — he would carry the mark of Good on his belly forever, and Malvel's evil would never be able to harm him again.

But Tom knew this wasn't his last battle with the wizard — Malvel would return!

Laughing with joy, Elenna ran up to the dragons. "You're safe now!" she called. She looked at Tom. "Do you think they understand what we did for them?"

"I'm sure they do," Tom said. "But what do we do now? Where exactly are we?"

"Check the map," Elenna said.

Tom brought the magic map out of his tunic and unrolled it. A golden dot showed where they were. "It's the middle of nowhere!" Tom groaned. "How are we going to get back home without Epos and Ferno?"

"We won't have to," Elenna said. "Look!" She pointed into the southern sky. Tom saw with a jolt of relief that Ferno and Epos were winging their way toward them over the snowy forest.

"Well done, Beasts!" Tom shouted, waving to the Beasts as they drew closer. "We'll get to ride home after all!"

Vedra and Krimon made welcoming chirping noises as Ferno and Epos landed gracefully on the snowy plateau. Tom ran toward Epos.

"You're better!" he called. "I'm so glad!"

Epos cawed loudly, her wings reflecting the moonlight as she spread them to show she was fully recovered. Ferno lumbered toward the twin dragons with kindly eyes. The twins' wings flapped and their heads bobbed as they rubbed up against the Beast's huge sides.

Ferno made a series of low rumbling noises and Vedra and Krimon began to climb up onto his back.

"He's telling them something," Elenna said. "I wonder what."

"I think he's letting them know that he's going to take them somewhere they can grow up safely — somewhere in the mountains of Rion."

The great dragon took to the air, the twins

clinging to his back as he rose in majestic spirals into the night sky. He turned, his black silhouette flying across the face of the moon as he headed south into the mountains.

"Epos? Will you take us home?" Tom asked the waiting flame bird.

Epos cawed loudly.

Tom looked again at the map, and saw a golden thread spinning out southward across Rion and down into Avantia — showing them the way home.

A moment later, a shimmering face appeared on the map. It was Aduro the wizard, and he was smiling.

"Well done, my brave friends," he said, his voice echoing as if it was coming from many miles away. "And you are right, Tom — Ferno will take the twins to a place of safety, and he will remain by their side and teach them the ways of Good and protect them until they grow strong. Now, my friends, climb up on Epos's back and come home to the palace."

"We won the fight against Malvel," Elenna said sadly. "But I lost my bow and arrows."

"Fear not — I retrieved them from the volcano with my magic," the wizard said. "They are waiting for you in the palace."

Elenna gave a yell of delight as the face of the wizard faded away.

Tom furled up the map and he and Elenna climbed onto Epos's warm and feathered back. Tom felt exhausted but he was in high spirits.

He clung on tight as the bird launched herself into the night sky.

"I wonder how Storm and Silver have been managing without us," Elenna said.

"They'll be disappointed to have missed the Quest!" Tom replied with a smile.

"We'll tell them all about it as soon as we get back," Elenna said.

Cool winds blew through Tom's hair as they sped southward over a snowy landscape that shone like silver under the full moon. Tom smiled. He had succeeded in his Quest and Avantia was safe. He didn't know if he would ever see Vedra and Krimon again, but at least there were two new Beasts who would be taught how to protect the kingdom; two pure and noble Beasts to join the battle against Malvel. And as for Seth . . . ? Tom shivered, knowing that they would meet again. Only time would tell when that would be.

But for now, Tom was going home.

Home to Avantia.

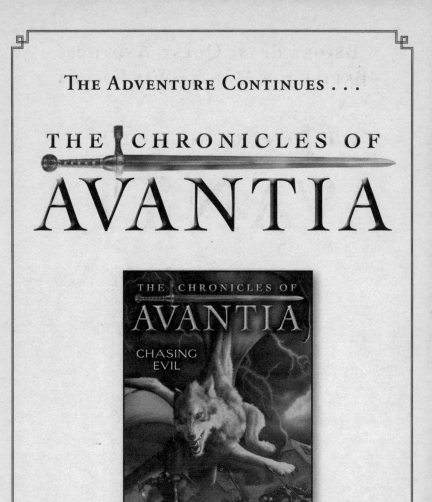